Happy Birthday, Ronald Morgan!

by Patricia Reilly Giff
illustrated by Susanna Natti

Viking Kestrel

JJ

VIKING KESTREL
Viking Penguin Inc., 40 West 23rd Street, New York, New York 10010, U.S.A.
Penguin Books Ltd, Harmondsworth, Middlesex, England
Penguin Books Australia Ltd, Ringwood, Victoria, Australia
Penguin Books Canada Limited, 2801 John Street, Markham, Ontario, Canada L3R 1B4
Penguin Books (N.Z.) Ltd, 182–190 Wairau Road, Auckland 10, New Zealand

Text copyright © Patricia Reilly Giff, 1986
Illustrations copyright © Susanna Natti, 1986
All rights reserved

First published in 1986 by Viking Penguin Inc.
Published simultaneously in Canada
Printed in Japan
by Dai Nippon
Set in Aster
1   2   3   4   5   90   89   88   87   86

Library of Congress Cataloging in Publication Data
Giff, Patricia Reilly.   Happy Birthday, Ronald Morgan!
Summary: Ronald thinks his birthday is going to come
too late for a class party, but he may be in for a surprise.
[1. Birthdays—Fiction.   2. Parties—Fiction
3. Schools—Fiction]   I. Natti, Susanna, ill.   II. Title.
PZ7.G3626Hap   1986   [E]   85-32303   ISBN 0-670-80741-9

Without limiting the rights under copyright reserved above, no part of this
publication may be reproduced, stored in or introduced into a retrieval system,
or transmitted, in any form or by any means (electronic, mechanical, photocopying,
recording or otherwise), without the prior written permission of both the
copyright owner and the above publisher of this book.

Love to
Deborah Brodie
P.R.G.

To Katherine Eliina
S.N.

"It's time for Show and Tell,"
said Miss Tyler.
I raised my hand.
So did my best friend, Michael.
"Me first," he said.
"Hurry," I said.

1

Michael showed his tambourine.
He banged it with his knuckles.
It made a lot of noise.
"What song are you playing?" I asked.
"You don't know that?" asked Rosemary.
Michael frowned.
"Can't you tell?
It's *Row, Row, Row Your Boat*."
I shook my head. "It's my turn now."

I went to the front of the room.
"I have something to tell.
Something good.
It's my birthday on Friday."
"Lovely," said Miss Tyler.
"Neat," said Jan.

"I have something bad to tell,"
Michael said. "School is over on Thursday.
You can't have a classroom party."
I looked down at my sneakers
and swallowed.
"I forgot about that."

"Don't worry, Ronald Morgan," said Billy.
"Classroom birthdays aren't so great.
I had lemon cake for mine,
and lemon makes me shiver."
"I had orange soda," Rosemary said.
"The bubbles popped in my nose."

I went back to my seat.
"I'm the only one who won't have
a class party," I told Michael.
Michael was still frowning.
"You're the only one who didn't
like my song."
I didn't answer.
I didn't want Michael to know
that I might cry.
Only babies cry about birthdays.

In the Music Room,
Michael shook his tambourine.
Mrs. Ling snapped her fingers,
and Rosemary danced.
"What song is that?" Michael asked me.
I raised my shoulders in the air.
"See?" he said.
"I knew you wouldn't like it."

It was time to go home.
Michael went to the front of the line.
I went to the back.
We didn't walk home together.
He went the long way
over the bridge.
I went the short way
around the corner.

At home my mother asked,
"How was school?"
And I said,
"I have two bad things to tell.
I have no school birthday
and no best friend."
My mother patted my shoulder.

We sat in the kitchen
and I had jelly and bread.
"What do you want for a present?"
she asked.
"A new best friend," I said.
I took a bite of my bread.
"I need a puppy, too."
My mother smiled. "How about
a game or a shirt?"

The next morning, we had Art,
and I sat next to Rosemary.
Her picture had tall blue sticks
with orange things.
I leaned over. "What's that?"
Rosemary turned her paper over.
"Private," she said. "Personal.
Don't look."

I drew a boy with a tambourine.
His ears were a little fat.
I held it up to Michael.
"That's terrible," he said.
"How come you made my ears like that?"
"You don't like it? Too bad," I said.
I changed the ears.
I made them even fatter.

After lunch we had Field Day.
I couldn't wait for the three-legged race.
But Michael went over to Billy
and I stood next to Jimmy.
We tied a scarf around our legs.
Mr. Spano blew his whistle.
"Race to the post," he said.

Jimmy and I ran as fast as we could.

Our scarf began to slip.

Michael looked back.

"No cheating," he yelled.

He tripped over a stone.

Jimmy and I stopped to

tie a knot.

So Rosemary and Jan won the race.

I sat under a tree to rest.
Michael was there with Billy.
They were talking about cakes with Tom.
"Chocolate," said Tom. "Delicious."
Michael shook his head.
"Whipped cream with cherries," he said.
"What do you like best?" Billy asked me.
I drew a cake in the dirt.
"Chocolate icing," I said.
Michael rubbed his foot on my cake.
"I knew you'd say that," he said.

On Wednesday I came in early.
Jan was the first one there.
She was sewing something.
It looked like a long blue ribbon.
"What are you making?" I asked her.
"Maybe nothing, Ronald Morgan," she said.
"Or maybe something."
She stuck the ribbon in her desk
and started to read her book.

Then I heard Michael coming.
He was shaking his tambourine
against his leg.
I tried to think.
"I'll bet that's *Row Your Boat*," I said.
Michael stuck out his chin.
"It is not," he said.
He slid down into his seat.

After math, we went upstairs
to the library.
"Time to tell stories," said Mrs. Cole.
"Let's all take turns today."
"My story is about wishes," I said.
"I wish I had a winter birthday.

I wish I had a puppy.
I wish I had a best friend."
Then Michael said, "I have a story, too.
It's about a boy.
He draws people with fat ears,
and he doesn't like tambourines."

I went to the Quiet Corner.
Only Miss Tyler was there.
She was cutting something.
It was gold and had lots of points.
"I know a story," she said.
"It's about two boys
who used to be friends."
"Like Michael and me?" I asked.
Miss Tyler smiled.
"One of them did something nice
for the other. Then they were
friends again."
I shook my head. "Michael won't
do anything nice."

Before we went home, I thought,
Maybe I'll do something nice.
I wrote on a paper
and left it on Michael's desk.

Dear Michael,
    I like boys with
fat ears. I like
~~tambou~~ tambourines,
but I don't know the
songs.   If I get a
puppy   we can teach
him tricks.

                Your friend,
                Ronald Morgan

The next day was the last day of school.
I hurried down the hall.
I could hear Michael playing a song.
I wished I knew what it was.
I opened the door.
"Surprise!" everyone yelled.
Even my mother was there.
She had a puppy in her arms.
Jan had a skinny blue leash,
and Billy threw me a ball.
Michael was smiling.

"This time I know the song," I said.
"It's Happy Birthday, Ronald Morgan!"

CONCORD FREE

CONCORD

MA

PUBLIC LIBRARY

DEC - 9 1986